DAISY
the Firecow

Viki Woodworth

Boyds Mills Press

To my Dad
—V. W.

Copyright © 2001 by Viki Woodworth
All rights reserved

Published by Caroline House
Boyds Mills Press, Inc.
A Highlights Company
815 Church Street
Honesdale, Pennsylvania 18431
Printed in China

First edition, 2001
The text of this book is set in 16-point
Usherwood Book.

10 9 8 7 6 5 4 3 2 1

Visit our Web site at
www.boydsmillspress.com

U.S. Cataloging-in-Publication Data
    (Library of Congress Standards)

Woodworth, Viki.
    Daisy the firecow / by Viki Woodworth.—1st ed.
[32]p. : col. ill. ; cm.
Summary: When no dalmatians apply for the job of
firehouse mascot, a cow named Daisy takes the job.
ISBN 1-56397-934-9
1. Fire departments—Fiction. 2. Cows—Fiction.
I. Title.
    [E] 21 2001   AC   CIP
00-101644

Daisy stood back from the herd and frowned at the other cows. "How can they look so content," she wondered, "just swatting flies and taking up pasture space day after day? Don't they know there's a whole huge world out there? Big teeming cities. Excitement! Adventure! I want to see it all!"

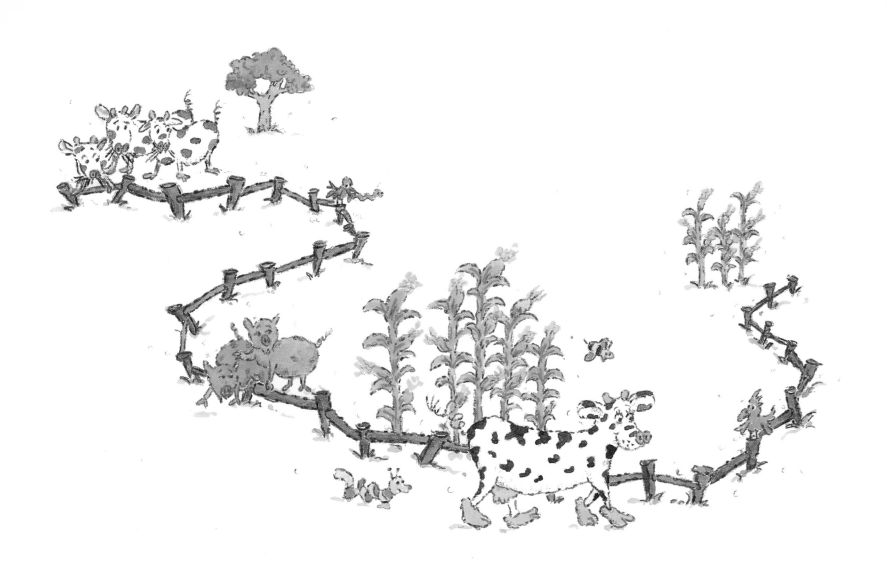

That very day Daisy left the field. She hoofed
along a dusty road until she came to a town.

"So this is it," she thought. "The Big City."
Daisy took it all in, her brown eyes open wide.

She arrived at a red brick building. On the wall was a sign that read:
NEEDED IMMEDIATELY!
FIRE STATION MASCOT
ARE YOU LOOKING FOR EXCITEMENT?
"Why, yes, I am," thought Daisy.

ARE YOU WILLING TO WORK LONG
DANGEROUS HOURS TO SAVE LIVES?

"Oh, yes!" thought Daisy.

"Oh . . . well, no, but . . ." Daisy looked at herself.
"I do have black spots. And I do want the job."

She knocked on the door.

"Yes?" asked a firefighter.

Daisy pointed to the sign.

"We were looking for a
dalmatian," the firefighter said.

Daisy pointed to her
spots, smiling hopefully.

Just then the chief walked by. "What is that cow
doing here?" he roared.
"She wants to be our mascot," said the firefighter.
"She WHAT?" yelled the chief

Daisy's big brown eyes filled with tears.

"Well, sir," said the firefighter, "a dalmatian hasn't applied for the job yet and, uh, she does have black spots."

"BLACK SPOTS!" thundered the chief. "She's a COW!"

But as he stormed away, he added, "As soon as a
dalmatian shows up, the cow goes!"
The firefighter smiled at Daisy. "You've got the job!"
he said. "At least for now."

So Daisy settled in as the temporary fire station mascot.
The first day she learned how to get into a fire fighting suit . . .

. . . and how to play checkers.

"A cow playing checkers,"
muttered the chief.

The next day Daisy and the firefighter rolled out
the old fire engine to wash and polish it.

As Daisy scrubbed and buffed she thought,
"How exciting! What a lucky cow I am!"
"Grrr," said the chief.

The day after that Daisy helped the firefighter
unwind the long hose and test it.

Then she practiced sliding down the fire pole.
"Mooo-eee! This is the life for me!" she thought.

"This is too much," said the chief.

The fire phone rang! The chief answered it.
"Fire? Russell's barn? We'll be right there!"

They zoomed away in the fire truck, with Daisy
hanging onto the side. "This is my big chance,"
she thought as the wind stung her eyes.

Russell's barn was all ablaze! Mr. Russell shouted,
"I'm going back in for my calf. He's too scared to come out."

"No!" ordered the chief. "That beam's about to fall.
It's too dangerous."
"Maaa," the baby calf cried.
Daisy had to do something!

"He's right behind that wall," she thought.
She gave the board a hefty kick. CRRUUNNCH!

Daisy peered through the hole. The baby calf was
huddled in the corner. "MOOO, MOOOO, MOOOOO!" called Daisy.
The calf came right to Daisy!

The others ran over just as she was pulling the calf
through the hole.

"Daisy!" they cheered. "You saved the calf!"

"Oh, thank you," said Mr. Russell gratefully.

The chief grunted, "We still have work to do."

They all worked very hard to put out the fire.
Daisy was magnificent!

When the fire engine pulled up to the station, there was a
big dalmatian reading the "Mascot Wanted" sign.
"Oh no!" thought Daisy. "This is it! No more adventure!
No more fighting fires! If they hire that dalmatian, my career is over!"

The chief marched right up to the big dalmatian.

Then he pulled down the sign! "Sorry, fella," he said.

"This fire station has found its mascot!"